ORCA'S SONG

Anne Cameron

HARBOUR PUBLISHING CO. LTD.

To John with
love
On your 5th
birthday

Auntie Maggie

Text © Anne Cameron 1987
Illustrations © Nelle Olsen 1987
ISBN 0-920080-29-4

Harbour Publishing Co. Ltd.
Box 219, Madeira Park, B.C.
Canada   V0N 2H0

Third Printing 1993

Canadian Cataloguing in Publication Data

Cameron, Anne, 1938 –
    Orca's song

    ISBN 0-920080-29-4

    1. Indians of North America — Northwest Coast of North
America — Legends — Juvenile literature. I. Title.
PS8555.A4307 1987   j398.2'089970795   C87-091137-6
PZ8.1.C350r 1987

When I was growing up on Vancouver Island I met a woman who was a storyteller. She shared many stories with me, and later, gave me permission to share them with others.

This woman's name was KLOPINUM. In English her name means "Keeper of the River of Copper." It is to her this book is dedicated, and it is in the spirit of sharing, which she taught me, these stories are offered to all small children. I hope you will enjoy them as much as I did.

Anne Cameron

Long ago, Orca was only one colour, black, and she lived, like all the other sea mammals, in the water, coming to the surface to breathe.

Sometimes she would lie on top of the chuck and watch Osprey riding the wind.

Osprey isn't any bigger than any other bird, but she is strong, and she flies higher and further, for longer periods of time, and she giggles and laughs at the things she sees below her.

Orca began to wonder what it would be like to fly in the air instead of swimming in the chuck. She watched Osprey swoop to the surface of the sea and rise back up again with Salmon caught in her strong feet, and Orca began to feel that Osprey was her special friend.

When Orca saw Osprey approaching, Orca would dive down to where Salmon lives, and she would chase Salmon up to the surface so Osprey could catch her food easily.

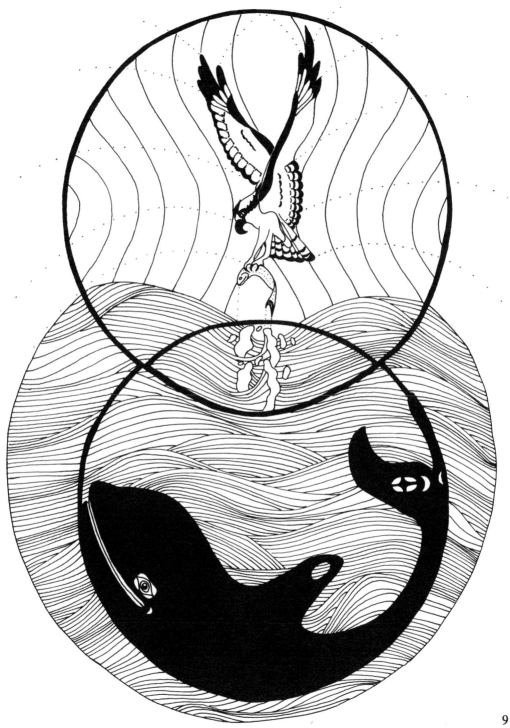

When Osprey realized what Orca was doing, she'd swoop over the waves, calling a thank you, telling of the things Orca would never experience: of snow high on the mountains, of small flowers in the meadows, of bushes thick with berries, and of sunlight slanting through the columns of the forest.

Orca told Osprey that she had never seen a flower, and Osprey brought a Foxglove and dropped it to her. Another time she brought Lupin, another time Dogwood, and when the berries were ripe, Osprey brought some for Orca to try.

Orca and Osprey became very good friends, and their friendship grew until they loved each other so strongly it was as if light came from their bodies when they saw each other.

But one was a creature of the air, and one was a creature of the sea, and neither could live in the world of the other.

Still, they loved each other, and love has a way of making sure it gets shown and expressed. Orca wanted so badly to know what it felt like to fly, fly as her love did, that she began to jump high out of the water, until there was no other creature in the sea who could leap as high.

And Osprey spent more and more of her time closer and closer to the surface of the waves, that she might be close to her love.

And one day, as Osprey swooped towards the waves, Orca leaped into the air, and for one moment their bodies touched, and their love was shown.

When their child was born, she was black like Orca, but with white on her body, like the head and belly of Osprey, and she could make piping sounds like the bird did, and she giggled.

Orca loved her baby and taught it everything a whale child should know, and Osprey tried to teach her to fly. But the new baby, though she could leap higher and further than her mother, and spent much more time out of the sea than any other creature, could not learn to fly.

Still, the black and white baby loved to leap and jump, to giggle and sing, and to play games of every sort. No other whale enjoys life quite as much as Orca, and every new Orca baby that's born has white patches, and they're different on every new whale, no two the same.

And because these wonderful creatures are the result of love between creatures of different worlds, they are capable of love for all things.

There is a place on the west coast of Vancouver Island where the rocks stick way out into the sea, and in the old days, the women would go out there at certain times of the year, in the spring and in the fall, when Orca is moving up and down the coast.

The women would sit on the rocks and play their flutes and whistles.

Orca does not hear only with her ears, as we do. Every inch of skin on Orca's body picks up sound vibrations, and she not only hears the music, she feels it as well.

And when Orca heard and felt the music of the women, she would swim to the place where the rocks stick far out into the chuck, and she would rise up, up, up, out of the waves, until she was balanced only by her mighty tail flukes, and, with most of her body exposed to the sight of the women, she would sway to the music.

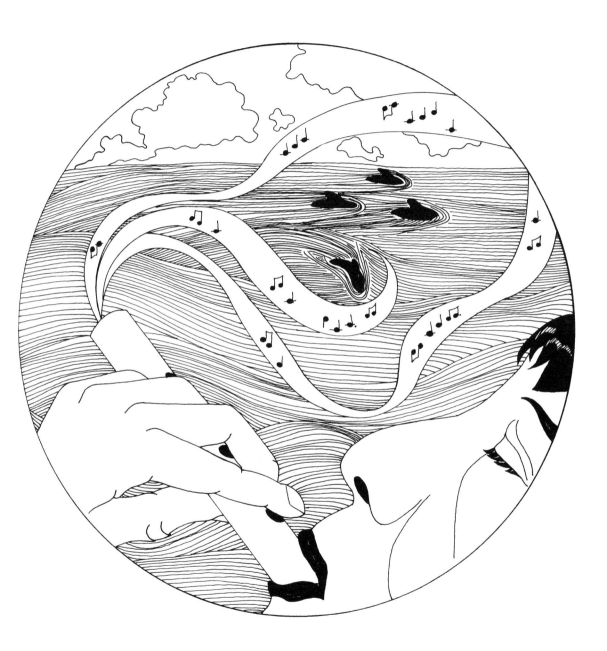

Then the women would hear the most beautiful of sounds, a sound so wonderful there are no words to describe it, a sound so full of love and truth it brought tears to the eyes, tears of happiness. The sound of Orca singing.

And the women would listen to Orca, as Orca had listened to the flutes and whistles, and sometimes, for a magical moment, the women would play their flutes as Orca sang, and the music of two different realities would blend and merge, and all creation would listen. It is said that at these times Osprey would fly up, up, up, her patterned underside exposed to view, and she would add her song to the chorus, and three realities would be joined in speech. And when this happened, the very rocks of the earth would begin to vibrate and hum, until all of creation, for a brief moment, was united.

23

Then, with a final sound, Orca would splash back into the water to continue her voyage. And anyone splashed by a whale has luck, and will have happiness, for this is one of the blessings of Orca, whose very body bears the marks of a love that found its expression and blended two very different realities.